Finding Elmo

Monique Polak

Orca currents

ORCA BOOK PUBLISHERS

Library and Archives Canada Cataloguing in Publication

Polak, Monique
Finding Elmo / written by Monique Polak.
(Orca currents)
ISBN 978-1-55143-688-3 (bound)
ISBN 978-1-55143-686-9 (pbk.)
I. Title. II. Series.

PS8631.O43F55 2007 jC813'.6 C2007-900247-1

Summary: Tim loves his job at the family pet store but he questions his father's leadership when a bird is stolen at a public event.

First published in the United States, 2007
Library of Congress Control Number: 2007920326

Orca Book Publishers gratefully acknowledges the support for its publishing programs provided by the following agencies: the Government of Canada through the Book Publishing Industry Development Program and the Canada Council for the Arts, and the Province of British Columbia through the BC Arts Council and the Book Publishing Tax Credit.

Cover design by Doug McCaffry
Cover photography by Getty Images

Orca Book Publishers
PO Box 5626, Station B
Victoria, BC Canada
V8R 6S4

Orca Book Publishers
PO Box 468
Custer, WA USA
98240-0468

www.orcabook.com
Printed and bound in Canada.
Printed on 100% PCW recycled paper.
12 11 10 09 • 5 4 3 2

For Julia Lighter, who's smart as can be.

Acknowledgments

Thanks to Rina and Angad Singh, Deena Sacks, Evadne Anderson and Claire Holden Rothman, all of whom read an early version of the story that eventually became *Finding Elmo*. Thanks to my dad Maximilien Polak for his careful reading of a later draft.

Thanks also to my friends in Australia, Vanessa Barratt and David Bock of the Australian Museum, and Trish Mooney of the Glossy Black-Cockatoo Recovery Program.

Thanks, as usual, to Viva Singer, who knows about everything, especially animals, and who always listened when I needed to talk about my story.

Special thanks to my husband Michael Shenker, for his love and support, and to my daughter, Alicia, who listens–and occasionally makes remarks–when I read my work out loud.

Finally, a big thank-you to the terrific team at Orca Book Publishers: publisher Bob Tyrrell who responded to an early version of this book; Andrew Wooldridge, who encouraged me to get back to it; Melanie Jeffs, whose careful, insightful editing helped me tell a better story; and Maureen Colgan, who gets me invited to all the good parties.

chapter one

I hadn't even unlocked the front door, and already I could hear them screeching. Would those two ever learn to get along?

"Get off the couch!" Winifred cried, her high-pitched voice carrying through the plate glass windows.

"Birdbrain!" Hubert screeched back.

"Quit your squawking!" I called, on my way to the aviary, where the birdcages are. "Breakfast is on!"

"Birdbrain!" Hubert screeched again. This time I laughed.

I love Saturday mornings. Most fifteen-year-olds would probably rather be sleeping in, but not me. On Saturday mornings–at least till Dad shows up–I run Four Feet and Feathers. Now that we've moved to our new location in Lasalle, it's Montreal's biggest pet center. If I sound proud, that's because I am. Dad basically started Four Feet and Feathers from nothing.

As I pressed my palm on the aviary door, I inhaled the store's familiar scent: hay, birdseed and ammonia, with a little fresh paint on the side.

Winifred crossed back and forth on her wooden perch, keeping a close eye on my fingers as I unlatched her cage door and reached for her food dish. "Get off the couch!" she shrieked.

"Winifred," I said, shaking my head and trying not to laugh. Winifred gets insulted if you laugh at her. "We don't even *have* a couch in here!" Her black eyes shone. You could tell she didn't believe me.

We'd inherited Winifred. That happens in the pet business since big birds like parrots, cockatoos and macaws–Winifred is a macaw–often outlive their owners. Winifred's last owner was an old lady with many pets, including a dog that shed a lot. Which explains how Winifred picked up the expression, "Get off the couch!"

Hubert, a gray parrot, was climbing the bars of his cage, watching as I filled Winifred's food dish. He knew his turn was next, and he wanted to make sure he was getting exactly what I'd given Winifred.

"Saturday morning special," I told him as I opened the fridge and took out a plastic tub of pineapple chunks. I added one to his food dish and another to Winifred's. Hubert stretched out his gray wings and for a second it looked like he was wearing a gray cape.

"Good morning," I whispered as I removed the old sheet draped over the next cage.

Elmo likes sleeping in the dark. He'd picked up the habit when he was living with his old owner, a sailor who'd brought Elmo home from one of his trips around the world. We'd inherited Elmo too.

As I stashed the sheet under the counter, Elmo stepped closer to the bars at the front of his cage. Then he lowered the top of his head so I could pet the soft tuft of black feathers there. Elmo is brownish black, except for a panel of bright red feathers on his tail. From the front, he looks kind of plain. But when Elmo spreads his tail feathers, there's no question about it, he's awesome. Though I had tons to do–the store opened in less than an hour–I gave Elmo a good scratch, reaching right for where his feathers met the skin.

Elmo's not a talker. Most cockatoos aren't, though when Elmo's excited, he squawks so much you'd think he was trying to make sentences. I knew he was enjoying the scratch because when I took my finger away, he followed my hand, pressing his forehead against the bars.

"Never forget the first rule of owning a pet store." Dad was at home, probably helping Mom deal with the latest disaster—yesterday the twins had caught pink eye. But I could hear Dad's voice as clearly as if he was standing behind me. "Don't get too attached to any of the animals, Tim. Remember, they're all for sale. Each and every one of them. As long as they wind up in good homes, we're doing our job."

The thing was, I was already too attached to Elmo. We'd had him since I was five. And though it might sound weird—especially if you've never gotten to know a bird—I was as close to Elmo as I was to Philippe, who'd been my friend since preschool.

I'd hardly seen Philippe since we'd moved to Lasalle. During the week he worked at a day camp near our old house; on weekends I was busy at the store. And so far I hadn't made any new friends in Lasalle. Mom and Dad said things would get easier for me once school started. I hoped they were right.

Thank goodness I still had Elmo. I just hoped his hefty price tag—two thousand dollars—would keep anyone from buying him.

It takes longer to feed Elmo than the other birds because of the padlocks. Elmo's an escape artist. Opening latches and padlocks is his hobby, the way some people collect coins or play computer games. Elmo will spend weeks using his beak to play with a lock, until he finally pries it open. Dad keeps adding more locks. Right now there are three on Elmo's cage.

A soft warm body rubbed up against my shins as I closed the aviary door. I reached down to pet Ginger, the store cat. Someone had abandoned her at our old store.

A marmalade cat, she spent most of her days in the front window, soaking up the sun in a giant cat condominium that was dotted with bits of her orange fur.

"Hey, Ginger. I'll be back when I'm done with the turtles."

Ginger purred.

Animals are easy. All you have to do is feed them and pet them and clean their cages and they'll be friends with you forever. Human beings are another story. Human beings are way more complicated.

chapter two

Dad usually sings when he walks into the store. Dumb songs mostly, like "How Much is that Doggie in the Window?" He also stops to say hi to everyone—even strangers—and to pet the animals. He's often got dog biscuits or cat treats in his pockets.

Not today.

Today Dad rushed by all of us and headed straight to his office at the back of the store. I was cleaning out the rabbit pen, but I saw him go by. When he slammed the door behind him, Cottontail went to hide underneath a log. All I could see of her was the end of one brown floppy ear.

I reached under a clump of hay until I found a small red wool ball. When I rolled it in Cottontail's direction, she peeked out from under the hay, her nostrils quivering. Cottontail's obsessed with cat toys.

"Everything okay this morning?" a soft voice behind me asked.

"Hey, Amy," I said, turning around. Amy's our bird girl. She looks like a punk rocker, but she's actually studying to be a vet tech.

"Birds fed?" Amy asked.

"Yup."

"Elmo still here? Nobody stole him?"

"Still here." Amy made the same joke every morning. She knew how much I loved Elmo.

"We're expecting a shipment of fledgling lovebirds. I could use a little help when they get here."

After Amy left for the aviary, I finished changing the hay. Rabbits don't just sleep in hay, they eat it. It would be like us eating our sheets.

Once I'd finished in the rabbit pen, I walked over to Dad's office. On the way, I passed the fish department. Trout, our aquarium guy, was skimming the deads, using a gauzy strainer to remove the fish that had died overnight. Dead fish are part of aquarium life, but they don't make a good impression.

I knocked.

When Dad didn't say anything, I knocked again.

"Who is it?" Dad sounded tense.

"It's me, Tim."

"Come on in." Though he'd invited me in, I had the feeling he didn't really want me hanging around.

Dad was hunched over his computer. There was a spreadsheet on the screen. That meant he was working on the budget. Realco–the real estate company that owns the Lasalle Mall–had offered us six months' free rent as incentive to move Four Feet and Feathers.

I knew Dad was worried about what would happen next month when we had to start paying rent. It was going to be way more expensive than the old location, and it didn't take an accountant to know that sales this summer had been kind of slow.

Dad hadn't asked my opinion about the move. It was his store, and I was just a kid. If he had asked, I'd have told him I wasn't worried about money. I was worried about the animals. A bigger store meant Dad had brought in more animals, but he hadn't hired extra staff to take care of them. That meant more work for all of us and less attention for the animals.

"Everything okay, Dad?" I didn't know what else to say. For the first time I noticed Dad's hair–it's the same brown as mine–had some silver in it.

"Uh-huh," Dad said, without lifting his eyes from the computer screen.

"Want anything from the food court? Coffee? Blueberry muffin?"

"Nah." Dad waved me out of his office. "Just trying to balance these books," he muttered. It sounded more like he was talking to himself than to me.

When I let myself out of Dad's office, I practically tripped on a piece of shiny black material.

"Rodney! You've gotta be more careful with that cape."

Rodney looked up at me with sad brown eyes. I'd hurt his feelings.

"Er...Phantom of Doom, I should say."

Rodney lips curled up a little at the sides. He loved it when people called him Phantom of Doom.

"Whatcha doin' here, Phantom?"

Rodney's eyes dropped to the tile floor. "My mom needed cereal. So she left me here. Said she'd be back in half an hour."

I'd never met Rodney's mom. But she must have bought groceries one item at a time, because she was always leaving Rodney at Four Feet and Feathers. I guess she hadn't read the sign posted out front: *All children under age ten must be accompanied by an adult.*

"Okay then, Rod–er...Phantom," I said, "let's go see how the Red Ears are doing."

As Rodney followed me to the terrarium where the Red Ear turtles live, his cape dragging on the floor, I thought he was kind of like a puppy. And if Rodney had a tail, he'd be wagging it.

chapter three

"What can I get for you today, Baba?" Mr. Singh asked. He leaned over his counter, his orange turban perched on his head like a flying saucer. Tandoori Palace was the busiest counter at the food court. Some people came all the way from downtown for Mr. Singh's homemade chai tea and creamy butter chicken. It was only 11:30 AM, but customers were already snacking on samosas or using their nan bread to scoop up Mr. Singh's famous chicken.

"The usual, please. An order of butter chicken with basmati rice on the side."

Mr. Singh dipped his ladle into one of the copper vats on the stove behind him. "That will be four ninety-five," he called out when he turned back toward me. His words came out like a song, his voice starting off high, and then dropping down a note at a time.

Mr. Singh pointed to a stool near his cash register. "Why not keep me company, Baba?" *Baba*, he'd explained to me, was Indian for *dear*.

Mr. Singh poured himself a cup of chai tea. It smelled of cinnamon and cloves. "Did I mention my great-niece Sapna arrives this weekend?" he asked after he took his first sip.

I took a bite of butter chicken. "From India?"

Mr. Singh nodded. "She's coming to help out at Tandoori Palace. It's hard for an old man like me to manage on my own. I told Sapna's mother I needed an extra pair of hands, and she told me Sapna's were available."

"Well, that's good news."

"You'll like Sapna. She's your age."

After Mr. Singh finished serving the next customer, he poured me a cup of chai tea. "My treat," he said. "Drink up."

Mr. Singh watched as I tasted his tea. "It's good. For tea."

Someone tapped their fingers on the counter. "I need three orders of vegetable curry to go. With rice and nan bread."

It was Mr. Morgan, the general manager of Realco. Whenever he came by Four Feet and Feathers, he had this way of acting like he owned it–running his fingers along the shelves to check for dust and commenting if service was slow.

He was our landlord, so I had to be polite. I put down my fork and said hello. Mr. Morgan was wearing a suit and tie and his silver hair was so perfectly blow-dried it looked like a helmet. Even his fingernails were buffed and polished. If he were a dog, he'd have just come from the groomer.

Mr. Morgan nodded. You could tell he didn't think I was important enough to remember.

Mr. Singh was quiet as he packed the order in a paper bag and stapled it across the top. "Thank you, sir," he said when Mr. Morgan paid his bill.

After Mr. Morgan left, Mr. Singh turned to stir one of his pots. "That man enjoys Indian food," I heard him say under his breath. "Almost as much as he enjoys collecting rent."

Mr. Singh's next customers were a couple dressed in matching leather jackets, each carrying a motorcycle helmet. "Hey, you're the kid from the pet store, right?" the guy asked me. His hair, which was dyed green and yellow, reminded me of a parrot.

"Yup."

He put his helmet on the counter and looked me up and down. "I need a guard dog to watch my Harley."

"You better talk to my dad," I said. "He likes to interview everyone who buys a dog from Four Feet and Feathers."

"He interviews everyone who buys a dog? There's gotta be something wrong with the dude." When the guy laughed, it came out like a snort.

I took a deep breath. "There's n-nothing wrong with my dad." I hoped he didn't notice how I'd stammered. "He cares about animals is all. He wants to make sure they go to good homes."

"Don't give the kid a hard time," the guy's girlfriend said, smacking him on the butt.

The guy snorted again.

The girlfriend's eyebrows were pierced. "How'd your dad get into the pet business, anyhow?" she asked. I couldn't tell if she was being nice or if she was really interested.

The guy took the trays Mr. Singh handed him. It looked like they were planning to sit at the counter too.

I relaxed a little on my stool. The girl was still watching me, which made me think she really was interested in hearing about the store. Besides, if there was one story I liked telling, this was it.

"When my dad was a kid," I said, "he hung out at this pet store near his house. It was the kind of pet store they had in those days. The cages were cramped, the animals didn't get much exercise, and people would poke at the dogs and cats through the bars of their cages."

"That's disgusting," the girl said.

"Well, my dad dreamt of opening a different kind of pet store. So when he finished university, he used all his savings to buy that old pet store and turn it into the first Four Feet and Feathers."

Mr. Singh whistled.

The guy wiped the side of his mouth with a napkin. "That's pretty cool!" he said.

Mr. Singh added some sugar to his tea. What he said next took me by surprise. I expected it to be something about my father, but it wasn't. It was about me.

"It's delightful," Mr. Singh said as he sipped at his tea, "to meet a young man who truly admires his father."

chapter four

"My hero!" Mom called when she saw Dad step out of the car with a bag of take-out. She was standing on the porch, a twin in each arm.

I decided not to mention I'd already had Indian food for lunch. I really liked Mr. Singh's butter chicken. But twice in one day was pushing it.

I followed Dad inside. I also decided not to say anything about Mom still being in her pink pj's. Or about the rings under her eyes. Or about the fact that we'd been living in the new house since April and we still didn't have any living room furniture.

Dad put the bag down on the kitchen table, headed for the sink and scrubbed his hands. I did the same, scrubbing my fingers till the tips were wrinkled. If we didn't, Mom would start sneezing. She's allergic to just about every animal on Earth–dogs, cats, birds, even horses. It's kind of ironic that my dad fell for a woman with animal allergies. Mom has to take two antihistamine tablets every time she goes near the store.

"Hey, Ems," I said, reaching for Emma and lifting her into the air. At first she cooed, but then she started wailing. That kind of really loud wailing that sets Jake off too. Which it did–about three seconds later.

It could almost have been funny.

"I'm exhausted!" Mom said. Then she wrinkled her nose. "And I think Jake just filled his diaper."

"I'm taking them both," my dad insisted, grabbing Emma from me, and Jake from Mom. "They'll just have to cry if they don't like it. Take a nap, Adrienne. Tim, you get dinner on the table."

"Do I have to?"

Dad gave me a look that said I did. I wanted to phone Philippe to see if he could come over next weekend. If he slept over Friday, he could help me open the store on Saturday morning. Only I figured now wasn't a good time to ask Mom and Dad whether that sounded like a good idea. And based on how things were going in our house lately, it probably wasn't.

Even heating up dinner felt like way too much work. Especially since I'd worked non-stop all day. Though everyone was always saying how cute the twins were, my personal life had gone down the crapper since they'd come along. Dad didn't have time to hang out with me, Mom was beginning to look like a bag lady and I'd practically forgotten what my best friend looked like.

Mom never did get that nap. She hovered in the kitchen, glancing at her to-do list on the fridge, while I took the plates from the cupboard. In the end, she was the one to change Jakey's diaper.

When the phone rang, Mom picked it up. "Honey, it's for you!" she called from the kitchen.

"Can you tell whoever it is I'll phone back after dinner?"

"My husband will phone you back," she said into the telephone. "Who's calling, please?"

She reached for a pencil. "Let me take your number, Mr. Morgan."

Not him again, I thought, remembering the way he'd drummed his fingers on Mr. Singh's counter.

"Did you say Mr. Morgan?" my dad shouted from the twins' room. "Tell him I'll be right there."

"My husband says..." Mom didn't get to finish her sentence. Dad had rushed down the hallway and picked up the telephone in the den. "You can hang up now, Adrienne," he said. His voice sounded sharper than usual.

When we finally sat down, Dad fed the twins–they'd just started eating cereal–between gulps of Mr. Singh's butter chicken. The cream of wheat dribbled down the twins' chins. Most of it landed on the floor.

I went to the sink for a rag. If I didn't clean up the cream of wheat, I was pretty sure it would still be on the floor in the morning.

"So, Mom...," I said when I sat back down. I wanted to tell her how Elmo had nearly figured out how to open the third padlock, but she'd fallen asleep. She was still sitting up, but her chin had dropped to her chest and she was snoring lightly.

"Dad," I whispered, "have a look at Mom."

On a better day, he would have laughed.

"How are those adorable twins?" Philippe's mom asked when I phoned. Philippe was out. He'd walked over to the dollar cinema with Thomas. "You remember Thomas, don't you? He lives around the corner," she explained.

I lay in bed, wishing I lived someplace else. Like my old house. I tried to picture my old room, the way the ceiling sloped, and the nature posters on the walls. Philippe and Thomas had walked over to the dollar cinema. You couldn't walk anywhere from where we lived now.

I heard the buzz of the electric toothbrush, followed by the soft drone of my parents' voices.

"I have to do something, Adrienne," Dad said.

"What do you mean?" Mom still sounded tired, but now, I could hear something else in her voice too: worry.

I shifted in my bed, straightening up so I could hear better.

"I don't know how I'm going to make the rent. Morgan is already putting on the pressure. He knows the store hasn't been busy."

I chewed on my bottom lip. What if Dad had to close the store? What would happen to us then?

"It's summer," Mom said. "Things are always slow in summer. People are away on holiday. Business will pick up in the fall. It always does."

"I've come up with a plan," Dad said.

Phew, I thought, relaxing a little. Dad was a smart guy. I should have known he'd come up with a plan. Maybe he wanted to hang a bigger sign outside the store or advertise on the radio.

But it wasn't that at all.

"I've agreed to start renting out the big birds," Dad said. For a second, I felt like someone had kicked me in the stomach. What was Dad thinking? "For parties and conventions. It's a good way to bring in extra cash–" Here, he paused for a moment. "They want Elmo first."

chapter five

"Tim! I need a hand with the lovebirds!" Amy hollered. Her hands were on her hips, so I knew she meant business.

I'd just gotten Winifred, Hubert and Elmo settled on the brass swings under the potted palm tree in the middle of the store, where they spent most of their days. Winifred was preening herself, her beak working so fast she reminded me of a bumblebee. Hubert was watching her, and Elmo was watching me.

I adjusted the swings, but truth was, I just wanted to hang out a little longer with Elmo. He hadn't even left the store and already I missed him.

The thought that my dad would be renting Elmo out like he was a DVD was driving me nuts. I'd hardly slept. There was no telling what could happen to Elmo. He might stop eating or catch a cold. And when I imagined the aviary without him, my throat tightened up.

I saw my own reflection when I looked into Elmo's dark eyes. "I'm sorry," I whispered.

Was I imagining it, or did Elmo look sad? Like he knew?

"Hey, pal, whatever happens, wherever Dad sends you, I'll be there. I promise."

"Tim!" Amy shouted again.

"What's all the racket about?" Trout asked as he walked by with a small plastic bag filled with water and two goldfish.

"I'm coming," I muttered, waving in Amy's direction.

Before I went, I scratched the feathers on the top of Elmo's head. "I promise," I whispered.

Each of the four fledglings was no bigger than a peach and just as fuzzy. They looked like they'd been splashed with green and orange and pink paint. Their pearly beaks were the size of fingernails.

"Hello, babies," Amy cooed. It was bad enough I had to listen to my mom fussing over the twins all the time. Now Amy was losing it too. You'd think she'd given birth to those fuzz balls.

I had to admit the lovebirds were cute. Amy had tucked a heating pad under their cage. Now, because we were cleaning the cage, the little guys were strutting across the counter. We didn't have to worry about them flying off since they still hadn't figured out what their wings were for.

"How are the fledglings this morning?"

It was my dad, but I didn't look up. Instead I scrubbed harder. So hard my wrists started hurting.

"They're doing well, Mr. Barnes. They had their food through the dropper this morning," Amy told him.

"Excellent."

When I felt Dad's eyes land on me, I didn't look up. I was giving him the silent treatment. But the silent treatment only works when the other person notices.

"I'll be in my office making phone calls," Dad said as he headed out the aviary door. He sounded happier than he'd sounded in a long time. Sure, I thought, he thinks Elmo's going to solve his money problems. If only he cared as much about Elmo. Or me.

"Something bothering you?" Amy asked.

"Nah, I'm fine. Hey, what's the red smudge on that one's head?" I asked, pointing at the smallest fledgling.

"Lipstick. A family was in yesterday. They totally fell in love with her. When I told them they couldn't take her home for two weeks, they insisted on leaving a down payment. So I dabbed her head with lipstick; that way, we'll be able to tell her apart from her brothers."

"Hey, Amy," I said, when we were scooping up the fledglings to put them back in the cage. "Ever hear of people renting out birds? For parties and stuff?" I was holding one of the fledglings in my hands, and I could feel the thump-thump of his heart.

"Nah," Amy said. "Never heard of it. Why do you want to know?"

"No reason."

The silent treatment hadn't worked. Keeping my feelings in wasn't working, either. So though I didn't have to pee, I headed for the bathroom at the back of the store. On the way, I stopped at my dad's office.

The door was half-open, but he wasn't there.

"I think he went to the bathroom," Trout called out. He was feeding the fish.

When I walked into the bathroom, my dad was checking out his shave in the mirror.

I looked for feet inside the stalls. I didn't want anyone else to hear what I was about to say.

"How *could* you?" I asked, looking up at my dad. When I heard my voice, I was surprised by how angry I sounded. I don't think I'd ever really gotten angry with my dad before.

"How could I what?" I could tell Dad had no idea what I was talking about. That made me angrier.

"How could you rent out–" I had trouble finishing the sentence. "How could you rent out Elmo?" It sounded like I'd spit out the words.

"How do you know about that?"

"I heard you tell Mom."

"Since when did you start listening in on private conversations?" Dad's eyes flashed and his whole face was red. I couldn't believe he was getting angry at me! He was twisting things. I wasn't the one who'd done something wrong, he was.

I tried to stay calm. "I wasn't listening in. I just heard you talking is all."

I was sure Dad would apologize for losing his temper and for his plan to rent out Elmo. I was sure he'd say it was all a big mistake and he'd changed his mind.

But he didn't.

Instead he walked right past me and pressed his palm against the bathroom door so hard it made a smacking sound. "What makes you think I need some kid telling me how to run my business?"

"I'm not telling you how to run your business. I...I just want to look after Elmo."

The veins on Dad's hand looked purple and swollen. "Now you're telling me I don't know how to look after my animals? Is that what you're saying?"

"N-no," I stammered. "It's just that I...I'm worried."

Dad dropped his eyes to the ground. "You don't know the first thing about worries," he muttered as he left the bathroom.

I knew there wasn't any point going after him. But I wasn't ready to go back into the store, either. My heart was racing and I needed to catch my breath. Dad and I had never fought before.

So I just stood there, staring at my reflection. I looked so much like him. Usually I thought that was a good thing.

But not today. Today I didn't want to be anything like my dad.

I nearly jumped when the bathroom door opened. I spotted the black cloak first. "Rodney!" I shouted, and for a second I sounded as angry as my dad had a few minutes before. "What's wrong with you? Why are you always following me around like some stray pup?"

chapter six

Not exactly pet people, I thought as I made my way through the crowd, balancing a tray of samosas over my head with one hand.

It was Saturday night and the store had been converted into a weird cross between a jungle and a ballroom. I'd never seen anything so tacky. I had helped Dad and Trout push the shelves of pet supplies over to one wall to make room for a giant dance floor. There was a cardboard cutout of a life-sized tiger at one end. The huge black strobe lights on either side of the tiger made it hard to see straight.

The people were even worse than the decorations. Take this one lady who let out a shriek when Cottontail jumped out from under the log where she'd been hiding.

"Don't worry. He's harmless," I said, offering the woman a samosa.

The woman took a handkerchief from her purse. She sighed as she dabbed her forehead.

The air smelled like the ground floor at some department store where those perfume ladies attack you with spray bottles. What I'd give right now, I thought, for a whiff of hay and ammonia.

Instead of renting out the big birds, my dad had come up with another plan to make money: He'd rented out the whole store. Maybe this was his idea of a compromise. We hadn't talked about our argument. In fact, since that day in the bathroom, the two of us hadn't really talked about anything, except basics like what had to be done at the store and what kind of take-out we were bringing home for dinner.

All the party guests were connected to Realco. In exchange for letting the company use the store for this party, Mr. Morgan had agreed to let my dad pay only half of next month's rent.

Dad had gone along with Mr. Morgan's plan like an old dog being dragged out for a walk. "What else can I do?" I heard him tell Mom during one of the late night conversations that I wasn't supposed to be listening to. "Soon I'm going to owe Realco so much money that guy can get me to do just about anything."

Why couldn't Dad stand up to Mr. Morgan? I'd put my pillow over my head so I wouldn't have to hear anymore. Why couldn't Dad put the animals first the way he used to?

So there I was, dressed in a penguin suit–a black tuxedo Dad had insisted on renting for me. I didn't even have a free hand to scratch my neck, which was itching something awful because of the starched collar.

I felt like it wasn't just Four Feet and Feathers that had been rented out for the night. I felt like I'd been rented too. Like I didn't belong to myself anymore.

Mr. Singh, who'd been hired to cater the party, was racing back and forth between the food court and the store. "These fancy people can't get enough of my samosas," he said, handing me another tray of the crispy appetizers. "The ones on the left have meat, the rest are vegetarian."

After the first round of appetizers was served, Mr. Singh gestured that I should follow him to the food court. His forehead was dotted with sweat. "Tim," he said, sounding more formal than usual, "there's someone I'd like you to meet."

I knew right away he meant Sapna. He'd told me she'd arrived earlier in the week, but that she'd spent her first two days in Montreal, getting over her jet lag.

I expected to see her standing behind the counter, but she wasn't there. At least not at first.

When she did pop up from behind the counter, cradling a copper pot in her arms, my first thought was that she didn't look anything like Mr. Singh. She had long dark hair that she wore in a braid down her back and her eyes were like stars.

"You must be Tim," she said. "I'm delighted to meet you. Great-uncle tells me we have much in common. There are twins in my family too. Mine are sisters. They have the same dark hair I do. Only not so long, of course."

When she talked, she moved her hands, and the gold bangles on her wrist jangled.

"Nice to meet you," I said, reaching out to shake her hand. Her fingers felt small and warm.

I didn't have to worry about what to say next because Sapna seemed to be one of those people who never ran out of conversation. It was hard to feel shy around her. "It was a very long flight from New Delhi," she said. "Fifteen hours if you include the stopover in Frankfurt. It's a good thing I arrived when I did, because I don't know how Great-uncle would have managed without me tonight."

Just then I heard the sound of someone snapping his fingers. It was Mr. Morgan.

He'd tracked me down at the food court. "I need two glasses of white wine for some friends of mine. On the double."

I wanted to tell him not to order me around, but of course, I couldn't. He ran Realco. And he wanted a kid in a penguin suit to serve wine to his snooty friends. "Look," I told Sapna, "I've gotta go, but let's talk later." Then I headed back to the store and toward the bar.

On the way, I spotted Elmo. He and Winifred and Hubert were perched on their swings under the palm tree. There were people milling around, gushing about the colors of the birds' feathers and coaxing them to talk.

"Hello, hello, hello," a bald-headed man kept repeating. He sounded like he was having trouble with his cell phone.

When I caught his eye, Elmo stopped preening himself and lifted one wing. I nodded and then, for a second, he shut his eyes the way he does when I pet him.

"Need some help?" a familiar voice asked. What was Rodney doing here? "My mom, uh, needed to get milk. When we saw Four Feet and Feathers was open late..." He was talking more quickly than usual. Was I making him nervous? Then I remembered how I'd given him a hard time the other day. He hadn't deserved it.

"Slow down, Phantom, will ya?"

Rodney cracked a little smile. "Hey, Tim," he said, "what's going on here, anyway?"

"They're having a party."

"Why would anyone want to have a party in a pet store?"

"Just what I was thinking."

"Are you sure I can't help?"

"Na, I'm all ri–," I said, but then I changed my mind. "See Mr. Singh over there at the back of the store? Could you grab that tray from him? Just don't let the samosas get jammed at one end."

Someone clapped their hands at the front of the store. "Mr. Morgan," a woman called out, "time for your speech, sir." Straightaway, people quieted down and headed to the dance floor, where a microphone was set up.

I grabbed two glasses of wine and hurried over to where Mr. Morgan was standing with his friends. The woman thanked me when I handed her a glass. "Richard," she said, holding her glass up to toast Mr. Morgan, "to a wonderful host and devoted friend."

"Why, thank you." Mr. Morgan sounded embarrassed. Then he turned to face me. I figured he wanted to give me a few more orders before making his speech. "Who's that child?" he asked, pointing at Rodney. "And why is he wearing that ridiculous outfit?"

"He's–uh–a friend of mine."

Mr. Morgan smirked. "I want him out of here. Now."

I tried to keep my voice low. Sure, it was Mr. Morgan's party, but Rodney wasn't causing any trouble. "His mom's just–"

Mr. Morgan turned his back and began walking to the dance floor. People clapped as he passed.

"Tim!" a small voice called out. Rodney was pushing through the crowd to get over to where I was. Why hadn't he gone to get the tray of samosas like I'd asked him to? And why was his face so pale?

Rodney's hand was over his mouth. His other hand was pointing at the palm tree. "E-E-lmo's not on his swing," he stammered. "Where'd he go?"

chapter seven

Problems have a way of seeming really bad at night when you're lying in bed and it's too dark for shadows, but it was morning and I wasn't feeling any better.

"You're telling me there's been a *bird*napping?" the police officer asked. He was jotting down notes on a pad of paper. From where I stood, the notebook was upside down, but I could make out the words *Four*

Feet and Feathers and *cockatoo–mostly black, some red.*

"This is the first time I've heard of a *bird*napping." The second police officer nudged the first one's elbow.

"He is a very valuable bird," I said, hoping this would make them take Elmo's case more seriously.

The first officer raised one eyebrow. "I see. How much is a bird like, what did you say his name was aga–?"

"Elmo. His name's Elmo." My nerves were shot. Elmo was gone. Birdnapped. What if he was locked up in some gerbil cage–or worse, a cardboard box?

"How much would you say a bird like Elmo is worth?" The police officer made a dollar sign on his note pad.

"About two thousand dollars," Dad said.

I hadn't been able to look at Dad all morning. I was too angry. This was his fault. If he hadn't rented out the store for the party, I'd still have Elmo. It didn't help that Dad was taking Elmo's disappearance so calmly. Wasn't he worried? Didn't he have a heart anymore?

The second officer whistled. "Two thousand for a bird? Geez, if I had that kind of dough, I'd take a cruise."

I felt my face get hot. "Cockatoos are like people," I said.

"Look, kid, I didn't mean to hurt your feelings," the second officer said. "Don't go getting worked up. Why don't you tell us some more about Elmo? He's black with a brown head, he's got some bright red on his tail feathers and he's almost a foot and a half long. Anything else we should know?"

"Here," my dad said, reaching into his pocket for his wallet. "Here's a picture of Elmo with Tim."

I'd never seen the picture before. It shows Elmo perched on my forearm, looking up at my face. Looking at the picture made me feel even lonelier.

"Does this bird of yours say anything?" the first officer asked.

I shook my head. "Nope, not a word. Cockatoos are smart, but they're not talkers."

"How much do those birds go for?" the second officer asked, pointing in Winifred and Hubert's direction. They were back in the aviary, confined to their cages until Elmo was found. If only Winifred and Hubert could talk. Really talk, not just imitate what people say. Maybe then they could tell us what happened to Elmo.

"They're more expensive," Dad answered. "They go for over three thousand apiece."

The first officer tapped his pen against the tip of his nose. "Looks like whoever took your bird wasn't much of an expert, or he'd have gone for one of those parrots. Can either of you think of any suspects? Anyone who'd want to steal your bird or cause trouble for the store?"

"Nope," Dad said.

"Me neither," I added.

The first officer turned to my dad. "I suppose you contacted your insurance company."

My dad dug his hands into his front pockets. "Well, actually...I was hoping you guys would be able to help us get Elmo back. Things here have been a little slow–" he hesitated for a moment "–and I haven't kept up with the insurance payments."

If I hadn't been so angry with my dad, I might have felt bad for him. Even I knew how important insurance was. If I were running the store, I'd never let the payments slide, no matter what.

The two officers exchanged a look. "We'll do what we can," the first one said, handing my dad a business card. "But you haven't given us much to go on. Let us know if you come up with any suspects."

Half-empty wineglasses had been left on the shelves, and paper napkins were scattered over the floor. But my dad didn't make me help with the cleanup. He must have realized I blamed him for Elmo's disappearance.

"Why don't you go for a walk?" he suggested. "See if you can find anyone who knows something about Elmo." It was the most he'd said to me since our argument in the bathroom.

I felt a little better as I headed for the food court. If the police wouldn't do anything, well then, I'd start my own investigation.

I heard Sapna's bracelets jingling before I saw her. "Great-uncle told me about your bird. I'm so sorry for you, although I never had a bird myself."

"The police just left." I stopped to clear my throat. It was hard for me to talk about Elmo without getting emotional. "They said they didn't have much to go on."

"Well, what are we going to do?"

I liked the way Sapna said "we."

"I guess we look for clues," I said.

Mr. Singh leaned over his counter. "Any word on Elmo?" He wiped his fingers on his apron, leaving behind thick orange streaks.

"Nothing yet," I told him. "But everyone liked your food."

When Mr. Singh smiled, the gold fillings in his mouth gleamed.

"I'm sorry I didn't get to taste the cake," Sapna said. "My mother says I've always had a sweet tooth. Even as an infant."

I turned to look at her. "What cake?"

"The party cake. I was loading a platter with tandoori chicken when I noticed the cake deliveryman. I offered my assistance, but he said he wasn't going far—that he was on his way to your store. I couldn't tell what sort of cake he was carrying because it was wrapped in white plastic. Personally, I like chocolate, bu—"

"Sapna," I said, choking on my words. "There wasn't any cake at the party."

chapter eight

My dad was on the telephone.

"It's about Elmo," I whispered.

"Just a second," he said, mouthing the words.

I shook my head no. I couldn't wait. Not even for a second. Why didn't my dad understand how important this was?

"Sapna saw a cake deliveryman walking into the store last night. Only there wasn't any cake," I said without stopping for air.

Sapna was next to me, nodding. "You've gotta let the police know."

"I'll call when I'm off the phone," he said, covering the receiver and waving us out of his office.

I scanned the surface of my dad's desk. His ledger book was open. I saw the edge of a business card with the logo for the Montreal Urban Community Police on it–a crest with a blue cross–peeping out from underneath it. I reached for the card and put it on top of the ledger book.

"Hey," my dad muttered, "don't mess with my papers."

I pretended I hadn't heard him. It was easier than getting into another fight. And right now, I didn't have time to argue. "Don't forget to call," I said.

Mr. Singh spotted Sapna and me walking through the food court. He was sprinkling some spices into a pot. "Sapna!" he called out. "I won't need your assistance until noon. Why don't you help this young man find his bird?"

I sighed as we left the air-conditioned mall. I'd forgotten how hot and humid it was outside.

"Can you remember what the cake deliveryman looked like?" I asked Sapna when we reached the sidewalk at the edge of the parking lot.

"He was tall. Then again, next to me, everyone seems tall. I'm only five-foot-one." I'd noticed how if you asked Sapna a question, she told you a lot of stuff besides the answer. "He was wearing a chef's hat. Not especially becoming on such a tall person."

We spotted the van at the same time. It was white with rusty spots over the tires and the words *Bob's Bakery* written on the side in curly letters. Next to the lettering was a cartoon of a dog wearing a chef's hat.

The first thing we did was check the doors. All locked. Rats! We tried peeking inside, but we couldn't see through the tinted windows. There was more lettering next to the picture of the dog. "Dog-gone good," I said, reading the words out loud.

"I wonder what Bob knows about birds that are gone."

The address was on the side of the car too. Bob's Bakery was out on Lakeshore Drive. "You said you like chocolate, right? How 'bout donuts?" I asked Sapna.

"We don't get donuts in India," Sapna said. "Other sweets, but not donuts. Have you ever tasted a gulab jamun? They're made with condensed milk."

I'd bicycled to the mall, and so had Sapna. We'd even parked our bikes in the same rack. Only hers–Mr. Singh had borrowed it from a friend of a friend–looked like it came from the Middle Ages. It was rustier than Bob's van.

We rode single file. I didn't have to turn around to check that Sapna was behind me. I could tell from the squeal of her brakes.

A bell on the bakery door jingled when we walked in. The next thing we heard was high-pitched chirping. Sapna raised her eyebrows.

"Cockatoos don't chirp," I told her. A brass cage hung behind the cash register.

Inside a yellow canary watched us from his perch.

"So you like birds?" a man's voice asked from the back of the store.

He wore a chef's hat. But he wasn't tall.

"Is that him?" I whispered to Sapna.

Sapna shook her head no.

I cleared my throat. "We, uh, saw your van at the Lasalle Mall and we wondered if–" I stopped myself. We wondered if you stole my cockatoo. Of course, I couldn't say that.

"My van?" When he clapped his hands, a puff of flour drifted to the floor. "It's been missing since yesterday. I filed a police report, but when I phoned this morning, they said it still hadn't turned up. You sure it's mine?"

"Dog-gone good," Sapna said.

The man grinned. "That's it, all right. Hey, did it look okay? Not too beaten up? The police figured some kids probably took it for a joyride."

"It looked fine," I said. "Except for all the rust."

"So tell me something," he asked, "how come you two came all the way out here?" He looked at Sapna and me, and I knew he was sizing us up. "By the way, I'm Bob. How about something to eat? On me. After all, you two detectives found my van before the cops did."

"We're looking for a cockatoo," I told Bob in between bites of my second donut. "He was birdnapped last night from my dad's pet store. Sapna saw a tall man wearing a baker's hat in the food court outside the store. He was carrying a cake–"

"Only there wasn't any cake at the party. There were only appetizers–and wine. Lots of wine," Sapna added.

Bob nodded. Even his canary, who had stopped singing, seemed to be listening. "I didn't have any cake deliveries last night," Bob said. "But the van was full of supplies–platters, a chef's hat, plastic..."

"White plastic?" Sapna asked.

"Yup," Bob said. "Listen, how about the three of us head for the mall? You might want to have a look inside my van."

"That's just what we were thinking," Sapna said.

"I'm no expert, but if you ask me, no kids've been in here." Bob was sitting in the driver's seat of the van, leaning forward to inspect the ashtray. "No cigarette butts, no beer bottles."

"What about this plastic?" Sapna pointed to the backseat, where an industrial-size roll of white plastic wrap was lodged in one corner.

Bob reached for the roll. "Hard to say if anything's missing. But the chef's hat is gone. I always leave it right here," he said, patting the passenger seat. "People like it when you wear a chef's hat. Makes the cakes taste better."

I crawled into the back of the van, scouring the worn gray carpeting. Nothing there but bits of dried icing and some loose change. Without meaning to, I sighed.

"You mustn't give up, Tim. If you give up now, you might never find your bird," Sapna said.

I didn't tell her she was making me feel worse. Why'd she have to talk about never finding Elmo? Instead I dropped my eyes back to the ground.

That's when I saw it. A piece of dark fluff on the floor behind the passenger seat. When I reached for it, I realized it was a feather, a long black feather with bright red speckles about an inch from its base. My heart thumped hard inside my chest.

Sapna crouched behind me. "Is it Elmo's?"

I picked up the feather and slid it between my fingers. I brought it to my nose, and for a second, I smelled pineapple. "It's got to be," I said.

chapter nine

On TV and in mystery books, kidnappers send ransom notes. They cut letters from newspapers or magazines so nobody will recognize their handwriting. Then they stick the letters together to make sentences like, *Leave a bag of unmarked bills near the mailbox and do not contact the police. Or else.*

A shiver ran down my back when I thought of the "Or else" part. It was bad enough that Elmo was gone. But, worse,

I worried the birdnapper might not know how to take care of him. Maybe whoever had Elmo wouldn't remember to change his water, which could cause a buildup of bacteria in the dish. Or maybe they would leave Elmo some place drafty. Even big birds were susceptible to catching colds, and if the infection went into his lungs...

It had been two-and-a-half days since Elmo's disappearance, and every time I walked into the store, I asked whether there'd been any unusual phone calls or letters. The answer was always "No." But then this was real life–not TV.

Keeping busy helped. When I was cleaning out the dog run–shoveling the poop, then scrubbing the floor with disinfectant–I was too busy to think about Elmo. Even rearranging the how-to-care-for-your-pets books helped.

But as soon as I stopped shoveling or scrubbing or rearranging, I started worrying all over again. The hardest part was walking through the aviary past Elmo's empty cage. Amy had covered it with the sheet, and I kept wanting to uncover it. It didn't make any sense, but I kept hoping I'd find Elmo inside, preening himself or rubbing up against the bars.

Even Winifred and Hubert seemed depressed. They were in their cages, ignoring each other. It was like they'd called a truce until Elmo was back.

"I know exactly how you feel," I told Winifred as I changed the paper at the bottom of her cage.

Hanging out with Winifred and Hubert reminded me of something one of the police officers had said: "Whoever took your bird wasn't much of an expert, or he'd have gone for one of those parrots." At the time, I hadn't bothered explaining that Winifred was a macaw, not a parrot.

Thinking about the police officer's words got me wondering about the birdnapper. Why *had* they taken Elmo, anyhow? There was no ransom note, so maybe the birdnapper wasn't after money. Which was good because I had a feeling my dad didn't have any unmarked bills to spare.

The police officer was right: An expert would have gone for Winifred or Hugo, instead. Unless...unless there was something about Elmo we didn't know.

Why hadn't I thought of that before?

Dad was out for the afternoon, tied up in a meeting at the bank, so his office was empty. I was in such a rush to get to the back of the store that I didn't notice passing anything on the way. Not the turtles, or the palm tree, or the fish tanks.

I heard the quiet hum of Dad's computer.

I went straight to Google.

I started by typing in two simple words: *cockatoo* and *black*.

I got nearly nine hundred and forty-six thousand hits. Wow, I thought, as I scanned the first page of websites that popped up. Most of the sites had been set up by pet owners–people wanting to show off pictures of their birds and hoping to chat online with other black cockatoo owners.

The fourth entry caught my eye: *Glossy Black Cockatoo*. Elmo's feathers were glossy all right. I thought about the one in my front pocket. I'd examined it a thousand times since I'd found it inside Bob's van.

But this time, I didn't reach for the feather. I wanted to keep reading. My eyes raced across the screen, moving faster than my brain.

"The glossy black cockatoo is native to Kangaroo Island in South Australia," I read aloud. Cool name for an island. For a second, I pictured Elmo flying across a cloudless sky, a couple of kangaroos on the ground, watching as he passed overhead.

My eyes pressed forward. *In danger of extinction, the glossy black cockatoo is considered priceless.*

Priceless?

How could Elmo be priceless? We'd inherited him from that old sailor–the one who'd brought Elmo back from one of his trips. Then again, maybe the sailor hadn't known either.

I clicked on the website.

What I saw next nearly made me hyperventilate. It was a photograph of a bird. Glossy black feathers, with bright red on his tail panels. But it was the eyes that got to me. Brown eyes, rimmed with pink. Eyes that looked right into you. The picture looked exactly like Elmo.

chapter ten

I was starting to feel like a human yo-yo. One minute I was up—like when I discovered Elmo was actually a glossy black cockatoo—the next I was down. Way down.

Like when I phoned the police station.

"I'll have to take a message," a woman with a bored-sounding voice said when I asked for Officer Leduc.

"It's about my bird."

"Your *bird*?"

I sighed. "Yes, m'am, my bird. Elmo. He was kidnapped, er...birdnapped and I want Officer Leduc to know it turns out Elmo's really valuable. Priceless even. Can you tell him I was surfing the net and–"

"Your number please," the woman said, cutting me off.

I gave her the number.

"He's working on a high-priority case." I could hear her tapping a keyboard in the background. "But I'll pass on your message."

Something told me Elmo wasn't exactly on Officer Leduc's high-priority list.

"Where'd Sapna go?" I asked Mr. Singh as I pulled out a stool in front of his counter.

Mr. Singh was using a mortar and pestle to grind spices, so the air smelled sweet and sharp at the same time. "Sapna has gone to Dollarcity for Styrofoam plates," Mr. Singh explained. "She insists they're bad for the environment, but the two of us can't keep up with the dishes. Especially on weekends."

He put the pestle down on the counter and shook out his wrist.

"Ever thought of an electric spice grinder?" I asked. "Or a dishwasher?"

"Bah," he said. I guessed that meant no.

I felt Mr. Singh's eyes on my face. "Any news on your bird?" he asked.

At least *someone* wanted to know the latest developments in Elmo's case. "It turns out Elmo's really valuable. Priceless, in fact. I found out when I was surfing the net."

"Are you sure?" Mr. Singh asked.

"Look at this," I told him, reaching into my back pocket for the printout of the glossy black cockatoo website.

Mr. Singh whistled. "Why then," he said, speaking more quickly than usual, "that would explain why a birdnapper would want Elmo."

I was starting to feel up again. Until Mr. Singh asked, "So what are you going to do next?"

"That's just it. I haven't figured that part out."

Mr. Singh made a clucking sound. "How about a vegetable pakora with some mint chutney?"

The pakora was greasy but good. "Solving problems is a little like cooking," Mr. Singh said, passing me a napkin. "It's a matter of taking one step at a time. When I make chicken curry," Mr. Singh went on, "I don't think about chicken curry. I think about onions and turmeric. I think about trimming every last bit of fat from the chicken. Good cooks–and I believe I may count myself among them–"

"You're a very good cook," I assured him.

"Good cooks understand that cooking is about the journey, not the destination–the steps, rather than the end product..."

I could tell from the way Mr. Singh's turban had tilted to one side that he was getting carried away.

In the end, Sapna saved me from having to hear more about chicken curry. The two bags of Styrofoam plates she was carrying were so big you could hardly see her behind them.

"Tim, will you please give that great-niece of mine a hand?" Mr. Singh said when he saw her. Then he disappeared behind his counter to make room for the plates.

It was 9:15 on Thursday night. "Let me guess," I told Rodney. "Your mom's just picking up a few things at Mega."

Rodney nodded.

We'd just closed the store, and I wanted to go home. It wasn't just that I'd worked all day helping customers, stocking shelves and cleaning out the animal pens. I'd been starting to think maybe Mr. Singh had a point. Maybe I needed to think things out one at a time.

I wanted to lie on my bed and review every single thing I knew about Elmo's disappearance.

But I couldn't leave Rodney standing out in the parking lot.

I checked my watch. "Did she say what time she'd be back?" I tried not to sound impatient.

"You don't have to wait." Rodney reached under his Phantom of Doom cape so he could tuck his hands into his pockets.

"I don't mind," I lied.

"My mom's always forgetting something. Cereal, bananas..."

All that was left of the sun was an orangey purple crescent. Soon it would be completely dark. I hoped Rodney's mom would turn up soon. She should have known better than to drop him off so late. Sometimes parents didn't act like parents. I thought of my mom in her pj's and my dad giving in to Mr. Morgan.

"You never talk about your dad," I said to Rodney.

Rodney hunched his shoulders under the cape. "I've never met him," he said in a small voice.

"Uh, look," I stammered, "sorry for mentioning it."

"They broke up before I got born. Mom says he loved animals, dogs ex-pecially."

"I guess that's where you got it from."

"Got what?"

"You know...your way with animals."

Rodney grinned. "You think I have a way with animals?"

"I'm sure of it."

For a few seconds neither of us said anything. I watched Rodney shuffle from one foot to the other, and I realized I wasn't the only one who had troubles. "You think Elmo'll ever come back?" he asked at last.

I made a gulping sound. I wanted to say I was sure of that too. But I couldn't. I gulped again. "I hope so, Phantom. I sure hope so."

Rodney was already focused on something else. "When's that building going to be ready?" he asked, pointing to an office tower Realco was putting up next to the mall. The frame was up, but only the first three floors looked finished. The metal scaffolding outside the building gleamed, reflecting the sun's last few rays.

"Not till fall."

"Then how come there are lights up there? See?"

"There aren't any lights up there," I said without looking up.

Rodney kept pointing.

I followed his hand. There were lights on. They were coming from the second floor. How could that be?

I got to thinking–to reviewing all the pieces. The bakery van was abandoned in the mall parking lot. Elmo—or someone who'd been with him—must have been in the van at some point, or I wouldn't have found the feather.

But maybe the birdnapper hadn't taken Elmo to the other end of town or the other end of the planet. Maybe Elmo was a lot closer than that.

A beat-up Volkswagen pulled up and honked. Rodney's mom leaned across to the passenger side and rolled down the window. Her frizzy hair reminded me of a dandelion. "You must be Tim," she called out in a high voice. "Thanks for looking after Rodney."

As I unlocked my bike, I took another look at the lights on the second floor of the office building. Somebody was definitely up there. And I had to do some more thinking.

chapter eleven

"How 'bout a ride to work today?" My dad's face was hidden behind *The Gazette* business section.

"Nah," I said as I popped a piece of bread into the toaster. "I'll take my bike. I've got stuff to do on the way."

My dad didn't ask what stuff. "Remember," he said, "no biking after dark. We were worried last night." He'd put the newspaper down next to his plate, but I could tell he was still reading.

I had the feeling I was supposed to apologize for worrying them, but I didn't feel like it. Dad still hadn't apologized to me. As I spread raspberry jam on my toast, I started feeling guilty for making my parents worry. They had a lot on their minds lately. "Sorry," I muttered under my breath.

Dad nodded.

When my mom came in, her index finger was pressed up against her lips. Which meant we were talking too loud.

My dad looked away from the newspaper. "Are they still sleeping?" he whispered. "Both of them?"

Mom collapsed into the nearest chair. "Both of them," she said with a sigh. I didn't think it was worth pointing out the dried baby spit on the collar of her housecoat. She reached for the coffeepot.

Dad blocked her hand. "Maybe you should go back to bed, Adrienne."

"Don't be ridiculous," my mom said, pouring herself a cup of coffee. "I've got too much to do." She took the lid off the sugar bowl. "Shoot, no more sugar."

"You don't have to call me ridiculous," said Dad.

"You don't have to be so sensitive," Mom snapped back.

I watched them glare at each other. Things were getting worse and worse at our house. I tried to calculate how many years till I could move out. Seven, maybe eight. I wasn't sure I could wait that long.

"We should think about getting a housekeeper. Even for one or two days a week," Dad said.

Mom winced as she gulped her coffee. You could tell she didn't like the taste of it without sugar. "Not until we can afford it."

It was only when I was biking along the lakeshore that I realized Mom and Dad hadn't even mentioned Elmo, or asked how the search was going.

I'd expected Sapna, but not Rodney. They were sitting on a bench outside the mall. I'd phoned Sapna when I got home the night before to tell her I needed her help again.

"I like feeling useful," she'd told me. "That's how I feel when I help my great-uncle. That poor man works too hard. Especially for someone his age."

"Hey, Phantom, whatcha doing here so early?" I asked Rodney. "Don't tell me your mom's already out of groceries."

"She had an er-pointment," Rodney said.

"A-ppointment," Sapna corrected him.

"Whatever," I told them. "Look, I need to fill you two in on the plan. I'm headed up there," I said, raising my eyes to the second floor of the office building.

Sapna frowned. "The building's not complete. There'll be no one there but construction workers. Why would they have your bird?"

"Rodney noticed lights up there last night."

Rodney's chest puffed up like a sparrow's. "What do you want us to do?" he asked.

"Just keep an eye out. In case."

"In case what?" Rodney wanted to know.

"In case, you know, something happens... or I take too long."

Rodney's eyes had turned big. "You're not going to disappear, are you?"

"Of course not," Sapna said, patting him on the shoulder.

As I walked toward the office building, I turned to look back at the mall. Sapna got up from the bench. "I'm going to check on things at Tandoori Palace," I heard her tell Rodney. "You keep watch until I'm back. Is that clear, superhero?"

There weren't any workers on the scaffolding, but once I got inside the building, I heard hammering coming from upstairs. The air smelled like white glue.

The ground floor had walls, but there was a gaping hole where the elevator was going to be. I looked around–past piles of two by fours, and bags of cement–until I spotted a stairwell. I stood still when the hammering stopped; when it started up again, I made a run for the stairwell.

I'd come up with a story in case someone found me. It wasn't very good, but hey, I was under pressure. I'd say I'd had a fight with my dad and that I'd run away. In a weird way, my story felt true. My dad and I might have had a fight if I'd told him all the stuff that was bothering me. That he didn't seem to care about Elmo or about how I was doing. That he was distracted all the time. That he wasn't the dad he used to be—the one who'd opened the first Four Feet and Feathers.

The stairs were made of black metal, and I could imagine the racket I'd make if I ran up them. So I walked super slowly, taking one at a time. I was headed to the corner of the building overlooking the parking lot.

Light streamed in onto the stairwell, but when I got to the second floor hallway, it was almost completely dark. I let my eyes adjust. A row of doors lined both sides of the hallway. The only light came from the cracks under the doors.

Now that I was upstairs, I realized I hadn't thought any further ahead than this.

Then I remembered Mr. Singh's advice: one ingredient at a time. Careful to make as little noise as possible, I started down the hallway. Then I heard voices.

Men's voices.

I ducked back into the stairwell.

"I don't like the idea of staying too long in this place," a gruff voice said.

"None of us do, Lyle," a second voice answered. You could tell he was trying to calm Lyle down.

"We should have left town after the heist like we planned." Then I heard a loud bash. Had Lyle punched a wall? I took another step back into the stairwell.

The word "heist" got my attention. Could they be talking about Elmo?

The hammering had started up again. *Rat-tat-tat*. I'd have to get closer if I wanted to keep listening in.

"Look," said the man whose name I didn't know, "the deal fell through. When Boss phoned yesterday, he said he'd have news soon. Said he thought we'd be outta here by the end of the week. On a plane to–"

The hammering got louder. I hadn't heard where they were going or what the heist was all about.

For a second, I saw myself the way someone like Lyle might see me if he found me here. Some kid crouched in the corner of a hallway, listening in on someone else's conversation. I shivered.

The hammering stopped and with it, the conversation. But then I heard more noise from behind the door. They'd turned on a TV, and I could hear the laugh track from some sitcom. But there was another noise too. A faint noise I could just make out.

Squawking.

My throat felt tight, like I was wearing a shirt buttoned up too high. It sounded like Elmo's squawk, only weaker. Wheezier. Sadder.

Part of me wanted to barge in right then. But then I remembered Mr. Singh's advice and the way Lyle had punched the wall. One step at a time, I told myself.

The men were talking again. "The bird's still squawking. That's a good sign, at least," the second guy said.

"It's a wonder," said Lyle. "Considering he hasn't had a thing to eat since we took him."

I tried to swallow, but it felt like something was stuck in my throat. Did I hear right? Elmo hadn't had a thing to eat since they'd taken him–nearly four days ago? Didn't they know a bird Elmo's size could die if he went without food for that long?

chapter twelve

I had to find a way inside.

I thought about knocking and telling them I was selling chocolate bars for school. But I didn't have chocolate bars and school had been over since June.

Then I got the idea of trying to break in through the room next door. If I could get in there, I might be able to climb onto the scaffolding and reach Elmo.

When I tried the handle it opened. Just like that.

There wasn't much to see inside. Bare walls and a concrete floor that felt cold, even through my sneakers. My eyes went straight to the back window and the scaffolding outside.

I was crossing the room when I overheard the birdnappers again. I tiptoed to the common wall to hear better.

"Boss told us not to leave the bird alone," the guy whose name I didn't know was saying.

"Boss this. Boss that. You sound like a friggin' parrot. I say we've been cooped up here long enough. Time to spread our wings. Besides, I've had it with leftover pizza." Lyle made a belching sound.

"What about the bird?" the other guy asked. "The doors don't lock. Maybe I should stay here."

My breathing quickened. If they left, I might be able to get Elmo. And I might not have to climb onto the scaffolding.

"What do you think the bird's gonna do? Fly home? Bird's in a cage, you doofus." I heard Lyle slap his thigh.

"All right, all right. Remember that vegetable curry Boss brought us? It came from this Indian joint in the food court next door. Little guy there is supposed to make a mean butter chicken. How's that sound?"

Lyle belched again. I figured that meant yes.

Way to go, Mr. Singh, I thought as I crouched by the door, waiting for the two thugs to leave.

When I heard the door close behind them, I made myself count to two hundred–slowly. What if they heard me from downstairs? What if one of them had forgotten something?

Once I reached two hundred, I headed next door, still keeping very quiet. I'd heard more hammering, and I didn't need the workers getting suspicious.

This room was bigger than the one I'd been in. They were using the backseat of a car for a couch. A half-empty pizza box lay open on the floor. But I was more interested in the hallway at the back. It had to lead to another room. And I was pretty sure Elmo was there.

"Elmo!" I whispered, "I'm coming!"

I heard a faint rustling of feathers. The pressure I'd been feeling on my chest lifted. My heart felt lighter.

I spotted him the second I walked into the room. He was slumped on a balsa branch in a cage about half the size of the one he had at the store. The cage was padlocked, which meant Elmo must have figured out how to undo the latch. Smart boy.

When he saw me, he opened his beak, but no sound came out. Then, slowly–as if it took every ounce of energy he had–he hopped down from his perch and pressed his brown head against the bars.

"Attaboy," I said as I poked my finger through the bars and stroked the top of his head. His feathers were dull and tufty-looking, and the bottom of his cage was covered with wispy brown and black feathers. Elmo was molting which wasn't supposed to happen until the weather changed at the end of summer.

I checked my watch. Three minutes had already gone by. I figured I had about twenty more till the birdnappers came back.

I could leave straightaway, taking Elmo with me, or I could try to feed him. Just then, Elmo opened his beak again. His tongue, usually a pale pink, was gray. He had to eat something.

On a table near the cage, I spotted a key and a plate of pineapple chunks. But pineapple would be too heavy on Elmo's stomach. I used the key to open the padlock, and then I unlatched the cage and reached in for the water bowl.

I dipped one finger into the water, and then I brought it up to Elmo's beak. His eyes were dull, listless. "Come on, boy," I urged him. Just when I was sure he wouldn't have any water, he opened his beak. His throat jiggled as he swallowed the first drop.

When I ran my fingers down Elmo's spine, I felt bones. I took some seeds from the seed dish, dipped them in water and cupped them in my palm.

Elmo pecked at the wet seeds.

"Attaboy."

It was time to get him out of there. There was no sense taking the cage. I pressed my forearm in front of his belly so he could hop on.

"We're going home," I told Elmo.

Just as he landed on my forearm, I heard a clattering sound. I thought it was coming from the scaffolding. Was it the workers? I was about to make a run for it when I realized the noise was coming from the hallway. Someone had dropped something–and now whoever it was was coming into the office. I had to move quickly.

I put Elmo back on the balsa branch and locked the cage. Then I put the key back exactly where it had been. My heart thumped so hard I felt it in my throat. I walked back toward the window.

"Where are those two blockheads?" someone asked from the front room.

Why did the voice sound so familiar?

It took me five steps to reach the window. I know because I counted them. A warm breeze blew up against my back. If I hoisted myself up in time, I could hide on the scaffolding.

"Lyle!" I heard the voice bark as I stepped out onto the scaffolding. I could tell the guy was on his cell phone. "I told you two not to leave the bird alone. Not for a second," he continued.

For a few seconds, I couldn't hear anything. Lyle must have been coming up with some excuse. But then the barking started up again. "Just get yourselves back up here!" the voice said.

Even after he snapped his cell phone shut the guy kept grumbling. "Curse that bloody Barnes for refusing to sell us the cockatoo," he said. "Especially after all the money we offered him!"

I nearly gasped. Why wouldn't Dad sell Elmo? Wasn't he always saying all the animals in the store were for sale? And with money so tight, I'd have figured...

That's when I placed the voice. No wonder it seemed familiar. It was Mr. Morgan.

chapter thirteen

I peered down between the metal bars to the pavement. I wasn't up that high, but I felt woozy when I looked down.

Who'd have guessed Mr. Morgan was a birdnapper? Wait till Dad found out.

I still couldn't believe he'd refused to sell Elmo. It was because of me, of course. He knew how much Elmo meant to me. Maybe I'd been too hard on Dad. Maybe he hadn't changed as much as I'd thought.

And maybe part of our problem was that I'd been changing too.

In the distance, I saw what looked like a black moth flitting its wings. Rodney.

Once he spotted me, he started running in my direction. His cape kept getting caught between his legs.

I inched up as close as I could to the wall and tried to focus on the bricks. It was better not to look down.

I could hear footsteps in the stairwell. Lyle and his partner probably hadn't had time to try Mr. Singh's butter chicken.

"Look, Boss," I heard Lyle say as he trudged into the office, "we were just downstairs."

Mr. Morgan's words came out like a hiss. "You know what a bird like that is worth. One of you was supposed to stay with him at all times. That was our agreement."

The voices came closer as the three men headed for the back room. I stepped away from the window.

"The bird's fine," said the guy whose name I didn't know. "Hey, there are seeds on the bottom of the cage. Guess he got his appetite back."

That seemed to please Mr. Morgan. "Good timing. The bird needs his energy. He leaves for Paris this afternoon."

Paris? They couldn't take Elmo all the way to Paris!

Lyle whistled. "That bird's got the life."

"His buyer's in Paris. Luckily I was able to arrange a new deal." It sounded as if Mr. Morgan was clapping his hands–applauding himself. "Our job ends once he lands at Charles de Gaulle Airport. Lyle, you and I leave in ten minutes. There's a van outside. Steve, Lyle will be back for you after he drops us off at the airport. In the meantime, get rid of all traces of the bird."

I scanned the parking lot. A gray van was parked near the office building.

Just then, I heard another whistle. This one came from the ground. "Shh," I said, mouthing the word when I saw Rodney.

It was too late. Lyle had heard him too. "Something going on out there?" Lyle walked over to the window until he was so close, I could hear him breathe. Whatever you do, don't look outside, I thought.

"It's probably just some bird," Steve said. Lyle stepped away. I'd been so nervous that for a few seconds, I'd forgotten to breathe.

I started climbing down the scaffolding. It was like a jungle gym, only harder because the bars were farther apart.

When I reached the ground, Rodney sighed so loud you'd think he was the one who'd been climbing.

I didn't have time to catch my breath. "They've got Elmo. You call nine-one-one right now," I told Rodney. "Give them that van's license number." I pointed toward the back of the gray van. "L-Q-Z one-two-four. Got that, Phantom?"

Rodney repeated the number like it was a secret password.

"Phone from Tandoori Palace," I said.

The van was locked. I ducked behind a nearby convertible and did something that's really hard for me. I waited.

My mind was racing. But I knew one

thing: Now that I'd found Elmo, there was no way I was going to lose him again.

I heard Mr. Morgan before I saw him. "Put that bag of cement in my van, Lyle," he said. I peeked out from behind the convertible. Lyle looked as mean as I'd imagined. His eyes were close set, like a bug's.

Lyle's arms were wrapped around a bag, and he stumbled as if he was carrying something heavy. I knew it was an act. That wasn't a bag of cement. It was Elmo. They'd wrapped his cage in paper.

Mr. Morgan unlocked the van doors and popped open the back. Then he opened the other doors. "With this heat, we'd better air out the car," he said loudly. In a lower voice, he added, "I don't want that bird getting heatstroke. I don't want to lose my investment." I clenched my fists. An investment. That's all Elmo was to him.

Mr. Morgan walked to the back of the van. He drummed his fingers on the roof as Lyle put Elmo inside.

I had to move quickly.

"Not so close to the window," Mr. Morgan told Lyle.

I thought I heard a squawk, but the sound was drowned out as a jet passed overhead. This was my chance to make a dash for the backseat.

There was a flannel blanket on the floor. Once I was in the van, I threw the blanket over me.

Perfect. Mr. Morgan and Lyle hadn't noticed a thing. They were too busy arguing. "Not so close to the air conditioning vents," Mr. Morgan said.

"I know what I'm doin'."

"If you knew what you were doing, you wouldn't have left the bird alone."

"Want me to drive?"

Mr. Morgan threw Lyle the keys.

I made my next move when the two of them got into the van. I hopped over the backseat into the back of the van. The flannel blanket came with me.

A few seconds later, we were heading to the airport. When Lyle turned on the radio, Mr. Morgan shut it off.

"You got something against techno?" Lyle asked.

I was glad they were arguing again. The more they argued, the less chance they'd notice they had an extra passenger along for the ride.

I had to find some way to get Elmo and me out of the van. Maybe Lyle would stop for gas.

I wanted to put my hand on Elmo's cage to let him know I was there. Of course, I couldn't. Instead I thought about Elmo–and what a great escape artist he was. What would he do if he were me?

Elmo loved unlatching things. If he were me, he'd figure out how to unlatch the back door of the van.

We were still on the side streets leading to the highway. If I wanted to escape with Elmo, I had to do it soon.

I wriggled over to the back door. Lyle and Mr. Morgan had begun arguing about money. "If you cut a new deal," Lyle said, "Steve and I should get more too."

I reached for the inside handle and

unlocked the back door of the van. Then I wedged a corner of the blanket under the door.

Now all I had to do was wait for the right moment.

"We had an agreement," Mr. Morgan told Lyle.

There was just enough blanket to cover me. I positioned one leg so when the timing was right, I could kick open the back door.

We were nearly at the ramp for the highway. I reached for Elmo's cage, keeping my arms under the blanket.

When Elmo squawked, I froze. I didn't want to imagine what Mr. Morgan and Lyle would do if they found me in the van.

I felt Mr. Morgan turn his head. "What's going on back there?"

"We haven't finished discussing money," Lyle said, hitting the brakes. The van screeched to a stop.

"Are you trying to get us killed?"

I thought this had to be the last stoplight before the highway. I bent my knee in toward my chest, and then I stretched out and kicked open the back door. I grabbed Elmo's cage.

There were cars everywhere. But what I remember noticing most was the blue sky and the sound of a police siren behind us.

chapter fourteen

"Now *this* is my kind of party," Mr. Singh said as he whizzed by with a tray of samosas.

Sapna was there too, dressed in a shiny green sari. She'd come all the way from New Delhi to spend Christmas in Montreal.

"I wouldn't miss this party for anything," she'd said when Mr. Singh and I met her at the airport. "It's not every day Four Feet and Feathers celebrates its first anniversary.

Did I mention my parents have been married for nearly twenty years, and they're planning a celebration too?"

We'd stayed in touch by e-mail. I'd even sent Sapna a message from an Internet café on Kangaroo Island. I'd spent a week there in October with my dad and Elmo—on an all-expenses paid trip courtesy of the Australian government.

The people from the Kangaroo Island Conservation Society had wanted to buy Elmo, but my dad said no way. Instead we'd come up with another plan. In the spring, a representative from the Conservation Society was coming to Montreal with a female glossy black cockatoo, and we were going to try and breed her with Elmo.

If that didn't work, I might have to think about letting Elmo move to Australia permanently. But for now, I wasn't going to worry about that.

This was a much simpler party than the one we hosted the night Elmo disappeared. Money was still tight, and I was trying to help my dad cut back on expenses.

We'd even begun looking over the accounts together on Saturday afternoons.

All we'd needed to rent for tonight were coat racks and a microphone. The coat racks were at the front of the store, loaded with parkas. Colorful woolen hats and scarves dangled from the pockets.

Even the canaries seemed to know there was a party going on. They were trilling their hearts out for the occasion.

"We wouldn't have had better music if we'd hired a band," Amy said.

"I just hope the fish don't get all worked up," Trout said, reaching for a samosa.

My dad adjusted the microphone we'd set up under the palm tree. Mom–she'd taken a double dose of antihistamines–had Jake in her arms. Emma, who'd just learned to walk, was on the floor, leaning against Mom's leg.

Dad cleared his throat. "I'm not much good at making speeches. But I've got a couple of things I need to say."

"First off, I want to thank you all." He lifted his eyes to the crowd. "You've been loyal friends and customers. I even recognize some of you from our first Four Feet and Feathers location. To be honest, I wasn't sure we'd make it when we moved to Lasalle. But here we are a year later." People clapped, but Dad kept talking.

"I need to thank the folks at Realco–at least most of them." Here, there was some nervous laughter, probably from people who'd heard about Mr. Morgan's arrest. Lyle and Steve had been arrested too, along with one of the construction workers who'd been paid off not to say anything about Elmo.

"Of course, I need to thank my wife for her love and support and for looking after our kids." People strained to look at the twins and me.

"But the person I need to thank most is my son, Tim." My face felt hot, but I tried to smile. I felt embarrassed and proud at the same time. "Parents are supposed to teach kids stuff, but I've learned a whole lot from Tim."

"I guess you know Tim's a hero. Together with a couple of friends–why don't the three of you come up here? Tim, Rodney, Sapna? Tim foiled an international bird smuggling ring."

People reached out to pat my back as I made my way through the crowd. They chuckled when they saw Rodney. He'd grown a couple of inches, so his cape didn't trail on the ground the way it had during the summer.

My dad put his arm around my shoulders. "Tim," he said, talking into the microphone so everyone else would hear, "somewhere along the road, I got lost. I got so worried about money, I forgot why I got into the pet business in the first place. You made me remember that it's not about ledger books and profits. It's about letting animals into your heart. The way you did with Elmo."

"Thanks, Dad," I said when the clapping died down.

Sapna nudged me. "Aren't *you* going to make a speech?" she whispered.

"Uh, sure," I said, feeling my face get hot all over again. I lowered the microphone. "Thanks to all of you for being here tonight and supporting the store. Dad," I raised my eyes to meet his, "you're the one who found a way to keep Four Feet and Feathers going when things got rough. You made me see how ledger books and profits matter too. And I want to say that whatever I know about taking care of animals, I learned from you. Now, there's someone I'd like you all to meet."

I looked out across the room for Amy. She was leaving the aviary with Elmo on her arm.

"Hey, Elmo," I said, and for a second, I forgot I was talking to so many people. They must have been following my gaze because they turned to watch as Amy stretched out her arm and raised her wrist into the air.

When Elmo lifted his wings, they made a rustling sound. A moment later, his sleek black body was moving over the crowd until he landed, like a jet, on my forearm.

I turned around so everyone could admire Elmo. "He's a glossy black cockatoo from Kangaroo Island–one of the last of his kind," I explained. "But to me, he's just Elmo."

Other titles in the Orca Currents series

Camp Wild
Pam Withers

Chat Room
Kristin Butcher

Cracked
Michele Martin Bossley

Daredevil Club
Pam Withers

Dog Walker
Karen Spafford-Fitz

Finding Elmo
Monique Polak

Flower Power
Ann Walsh

Hypnotized
Don Trembath

Laggan Lard Butts
Eric Walters

Mirror Image
K.L. Denman

Pigboy
Vicki Grant

Queen of the Toilet Bowl
Frieda Wishinsky

See No Evil
Diane Young

Sewer Rats
Sigmund Brouwer

Spoiled Rotten
Dayle Campbell Gaetz

Sudden Impact
Lesley Choyce

Swiped
Michele Martin Bossley

Wired
Sigmund Brouwer

When award-winning author Monique Polak was a kid, her best friend was her budgie, Nervous Thompson Williamson. Monique is the popular author of many books for children and young adults, including *Home Invasion* and *No More Pranks* in the Orca Soundings series. Monique lives in Montreal, Quebec.